For Russell, who had
a Good Idea.

Aug. 29/94

To Benjie,

Remember you didn't want me to
buy this book for you, but now you
enjoy reading it so much.

Love
Shifra

HERBERT: THE BLOTCHY GREAT SNAPPER

Written and Illustrated by Roz Wolseley-Charles

edited by Jill Bray

Pipe Elm Publications
Leigh Sinton, Malvern,
Worcestershire, WR13 5EA

Copyright: Roz Wolseley-Charles © 1984

Photo set by Juno Enterprises, Malvern

CHAPTER 1

There was a fish.

He was fat and round and he lay all day at the bottom of the river, minding his own business. The mud was cool and deep and food came floating by in large quantities, so the fish (whose name was Herbert) had a most comfortable life and never expected it to be any different.

But most good things come to an end, and by the time Herbert had his fifth birthday—which he celebrated by eating two of his cousins called Yvonne and Eric—the river started to change.

Herbert did not know, of course, what was happening on the riverbank, but far above his head people began to arrive. They wore yellow safety-helmets and they brought digging machines and pile drivers and a lot of other equipment. They were going to build a bridge right over the river, exactly where Herbert lay in his favourite place.

The first thing he knew about it was a lot of upheaval, and his nice quiet mud was churned to a brown, soupy mess. Herbert was tipped out of his home and hit on the head. It brought on a terrible migraine, but he didn't have much time to worry about that as he tumbled head-over-tail in the surging water.

Machinery came down onto the river bed. Voices shouted. Engines roared. Generators pounded. The noise in a very short while was absolutely horrific.

Herbert was washed out. Caught in about a dozen undertows, he was helpless. His relations were with him, but he had never really got on with them, and their company now did nothing to cheer him. They were swept here and there until at last they all managed to reach a quieter place further downstream.

Herbert collapsed into a bed of waterweeds and tried to compose himself. His headache was terrible, but after a rest he felt better, and then he saw his Aunt Edith swimming by. He was suddenly hungry. He watched Aunt Edith closely and, as she swam past his hiding place, he pounced on her and chewed her up. Then he went to sleep.

Next morning, very early, he slid out of his waterweeds and swam up-river. He came to where his old home had been, but everything was changed. His shelter had gone; so had the plants and caddis-flies, the waterboatmen and all the little fish. The river was empty except for great pieces of machinery waiting for the engineers to start work.

Herbert surfaced and looked around. Only one man was on the bank. He was a Conservationist; his name was Mr. Hathaway and he was examining the river's edge. Herbert made a plop! as he dived for cover, but not before Mr. Hathaway had seen him and become extremely interested.

Mr. Hathaway brought a huge net. He waded into the shallows and he waited until Herbert surfaced again—then he scooped the net under poor Herbert, and that was that. Herbert was dumped into a plastic bucket and the Site Engineer came to see him because Mr. Hathaway was so excited.

'What is *that*?' asked the Site Engineer.

'That,' said Mr. Hathaway, 'is a Blotchy Great Snapper!'

Herbert lay low and watched. He was rather pleased to hear of his new title—he thought it had class. Also, it explained the reason for the quantities of teeth he had. He looked at Mr. Hathaway and the Site Engineer. Their fingers kept coming nearer as they talked and pointed at him. The fingers were large and sausagey and altogether very tasty-looking, so, when Mr. Hathaway prodded at Herbert, it took him no time at all to leap upwards and take a huge bite out of the meaty finger.

'Yow!' yelled Mr. Hathaway. 'Yow!'

'I can see why it's called a Blotchy Great Snapper,' said the Site Engineer, hiding a grin.

Herbert sank down in his bucket and chewed his breakfast. It was tougher than Yvonne or Eric or Aunt Edith, but still very acceptable.

'They are cannibals really,' said Mr. Hathaway, wrapping a handkerchief round his damaged finger. 'But they are Extremely Rare.'

'So that is what I am,' thought Herbert. 'No wonder my cousins and dear Auntie tasted so good.'

They loaded him onto the Land Rover. Mr. Hathaway took him to the Water Authority's Offices. Herbert lay still and thought. He had a lot to think about. He had found out he was a Blotchy Great Snapper; he was a cannibal and he was Extremely Rare. But he had lost his home, his river, and he had another migraine coming on.

'Someone,' thought Herbert, 'is going to pay for this.'

Two days later the Television people arrived. They loaded Herbert (in a brand new tank) into a van and took him to the television studios.

Herbert watched through the glass.

The Angling Correspondent arrived to introduce Herbert to the public. He wore a check suit of dubious taste stretched over his fat stomach. He leaned over Herbert's tank and poked at him.

'Ha-ha, me lad!' said the Angling Correspondent. 'Come on, there! Move about a bit!'

Herbert moved. He shot out of the tank like a guided missile and he fastened his teeth on the Angling Correspondent's finger. Then he fell back into the water taking a large piece of the Angling Correspondent's first finger with him.

'Scream!' went the Angling Correspondent. 'Scream! Scream!'

'What is going on?' yelled Mr. Hathaway, rushing up.

'It's your blurry fish!' shouted the Angling Correspondent. 'It's worse than a piranha! Look what it's done to me!'

'Serve you right and all,' thought Herbert, reflectively chewing. 'Poking persons about. It is not polite.'

They led the Angling Correspondent away to First Aid and they put a plaster on his finger. He wanted his arm in a sling but they told him it would not look good On Camera.

So he sat in his Interview Chair and hated Herbert.

The Programme was a great success. No one had ever seen a Blotchy Great Snapper before because they are so Extremely Rare. Herbert was a sensation. He ate all the bits of meat they dropped in the tank and displayed his teeth splendidly.

There was no chance to leap out again, as everyone took care to keep at a safe distance. He liked the warm lights, and the noise was bearable.

'This is the life,' thought Herbert. 'I shall be a TV Celebrity. How can I make a career of it?'

At that very moment the Angling Correspondent was introducing the famous explorer and wild life expert, David Smith. Mr. Smith looked at Herbert and said, 'Well! well! Isn't he marvellous?'

'Yes, I am,' thought Herbert.

'He would be a wow in my next series, "Life in Water",' said Mr. Smith.

'Yes, I would,' thought Herbert.

'A pity we haven't any more like him,' said Mr. Smith.

'If you had more like me, I would make short work of 'em,' thought Herbert.

'Is he *really* so violent?' said Mr. Smith, and, before anyone could stop him, he put his whole hand in the water.

Herbert was no fool. He swam over to the hand and rubbed his back against it. He was revolted, really, but he kept his mouth firmly under control.

'I *will* be a Star,' thought Herbert through clenched teeth.

Mr. Smith was delighted. The Angling Correspondent was livid. Mr. Hathaway was pretty pleased with Herbert's success, but sad at having to part with him. Herbert's tank with Herbert in it went home with Mr. Smith in a taxi, paid for by the television studios.

After that, the river could go and hang itself for all Herbert cared. He had a super tank, loads of food and a Great Career. He appeared in many shows such as the famous "Life in Water", when he amazed all viewers with the speed at which he could eat other fish. One he recognised; she was his second cousin, Gloria, but he could not let family feelings stand in his way. Anyhow, she made a nice change from chopped beef.

Now Herbert has a Star on the dressing room he shares with Mr. Smith. He travels the world and meets famous people. He is well pleased with the

way things turned out.

And he could not care less about the dear old river. That is just as well.

It's polluted.

CHAPTER TWO

Herbert, the Blotchy Great Snapper who was also Extremely Rare, rested on the bottom of his tank and thought deeply. His career was going quite nicely with Mr. Smith in charge, and many engagements were booked for Herbert to do his stuff for the Public. His tank was the latest thing in comfort, with coloured gravel at the bottom and large green waterweeds at the top. His diet was mainly chopped beef and ants' eggs and it was this that caused Herbert to cogitate so deeply. It seemed to be a bit monotonous, and he felt a change now and then would be welcome, but how to get the message across to Mr. Smith was beyond his immediate means. However, he watched for an opportunity to present itself and he was confident one would occur.

It did.

Mr. Smith arrived one morning, smiling all over his face.

'Goodness,' thought Herbert, as Mr. Smith peered through the glass at him. 'I am thankful I cannot smile like that. His mouth stretches halfway round his earholes!'

'Hey, boy!' sang Mr. Smith. 'We are off to do a programme in France! France! Home of good cooking! What d'you think of that, eh?'

'Good cooking,' thought Herbert, 'is not something I am interested in.

I enjoy my meals raw and preferably kicking.'

And he sank to the tank's bottom and chewed gloomily on a few ants' eggs.

The day soon came when Mr. Smith and Herbert set sail for France in the Hovercraft. Never in his whole life had Herbert felt so ill. The water outside heaved up and down and so did the water in his tank. If ever a fish was seasick, it was poor Herbert. Mr. Smith wasn't much better.

They were truly thankful to disembark and to go to a hotel for a rest.

Next day things looked brighter. A taxi called for them and they were taken to the television studios where they were welcomed and shown around the place. They also met the producer of their programme.

'Ah-ha!' he exclaimed, 'so this ees zee great 'Erbert! Mon Dieu! What an 'uge poisson!'

'Poison yourself, mate,' thought Herbert. 'But keep out of my territory.'

The programme had another wild-life expert, who was to demonstrate his particular interest in water-creatures, so Herbert waited with great curiosity to see what kind of fish or insects would be shown. When he saw what the French expert had in his little glass vivarium, Herbert couldn't believe his eyes.

FROGS!!!

Lovely, green, jumpy, twitchy FROGS!

Oh, how Herbert loved frogs! He used to eat them by the kilo in the dear

old river, and it seemed a lifetime since they had been on his menu and; in any case, these French frogs were so fat and so green and so shiny—oooh!

From that moment he concentrated on one thing only—FROGS FOR DINNER!

The producer made Mr. Smith wait in second place, and the French expert went on camera first with his French frogs.

Herbert swam slowly to the top of the water and looked around. He saw the cameras, the lights, Mr. Smith waiting patiently, and he saw the producer's hand resting casually on the edge of his tank. There was a splendid gold cuff-link in his shirt sleeve. It glittered. So did Herbert's eyes!

He slid through the waterweeds, positioned himself carefully and then he shot like a fat arrow up into the air; his teeth snapped round the cuff-link

and Herbert with his treasure flopped back into the tank with a terrific splash that sprayed everybody for yards around.

'Sacré bleu!' screamed the producer, 'zat foul poisson 'as eaten mon cufflinque d'or! Give eet back, you English monstair!'

'Nuts to you,' thought Herbert. Mr. Smith jumped up and ran across to try to soothe the producer, but that excitable gentleman was flailing around like a windmill and exactly what Herbert had hoped for actually happened. The producer knocked over the frogs' glass vivarium and the frogs—which were hot and dry under the studio lights—jumped joyfully across the tabletop towards the lovely water they could smell in Herbert's tank.

'Non! Non!' shrieked the French expert. 'Ah, sacré nom d'un chien! Mes petites grenouilles!'

'Language,' thought Herbert.

He waited in the waterweeds as the frogs jumped over the table, skilfully avoiding the French technicians. First one, then another and then several more arrived in the tank. And the welcoming committee swam to meet them with his mouth wide open.

The frogs were delicious! Herbert had a real taste of French food that evening.

Meanwhile, pandemonium reigned in the studio; the producer was swearing to murder Herbert; the French wildlife expert was sobbing his heart out because the frogs were rare ones which he had brought back from Zaire and he certainly didn't fancy another trip for fresh supplies; Mr. Smith was desperately attempting to hook up the cuff-link out of Herbert's tank without attracting Herbert's attention; the technicians were trying to wind up the programme as fast as they could in the midst of broken glass, spilt water and hysteria; and altogether Herbert considered it to be a very messy affair and not at all like the dear old British Television.

'I will murdair 'eem! 'E 'ave ruin mon career! Let me at 'eem!' screamed the producer.

'Get off,' thought Herbert, 'I have Diplomatic Immunity. And even if I haven't, one false move from you and I will take your 'and off at ze wriste.'

Well, of course, after that Mr. Smith got himself and Herbert out of the studio, the hotel, the Hovercraft and out of France (in that order) as quickly as he could.

Back in England he rang up Mr. Hathaway, whose career had been doing very nicely. He had become a Scientific Officer with his own Research Laboratory, but he missed Herbert terribly. Just imagine his delight when Mr. Smith asked if he would like to have Herbert back again, as Mr. Smith was going abroad and Herbert would not be welcome on the trip.

'Golly, *yes!*' said Mr. Hathaway joyfully. 'I'd *love* to have him back! I've got just the place for him in my lab. I'll fetch him tomorrow'

Herbert listened with his face pressed against the glass. It sounded good to him.

Mr. Smith said thanks and goodbye, then he put the phone down and walked over to where Herbert was watching. Mr. Smith drew back his fist. Herbert retreated into the weeds, keeping a careful eye on Mr. Smith.

'YOU!' said Mr. Smith, 'after all I've done for you! I take you all over the place; I make you famous; I feed you best beef at heaven knows how much a pound, and what do *you* do? You ruin my Continental Début, *that's* what you do!'

'Naughty,' thought Herbert. 'Control yourself. All this Gallic temperament has got to you.'

'Hathaway can have you and welcome!' said Mr. Smith bitterly, and he slammed out of the door.

Mr. Hathaway came next day to get Herbert.

'Poor old lad! You can't have been cleaned out for several days!' he said sympathetically.

'Just as well,' thought Herbert. He had discovered a disembodied frog's leg in the water weeds and was chewing on it appreciatively. His little French friend's remnant tasted delicious.

'There are altogether too many French people in France for comfort,' thought Herbert, 'but the stories about the food are certainly true. The frogs are *great*. I wonder if I'll ever get a chance at some snails?'

Mr. Hathaway slopped downstairs with the tank, and at the door he put it down to wipe his forehead.

'By golly, Herbert!' he gasped, 'you must have put on weight! What *have* you been eating?'

Herbert burped.

CHAPTER 3

Herbert was on his own in his tank in the laboratory. He was alone quite often, as Mr. Hathaway was busy on other projects and Herbert's career as a TV Celebrity had more or less slithered to a stop just lately.

He was bored. He liked excitement, and the only remotely exciting thing in the lab. was the television which Mr. Hathaway had installed on a bench to keep Herbert company. It was switched on every morning by a lab. assistant and it stayed on until the little bright spot faded out at night. Herbert grew quite attached to the bright spot. As entertainment value it didn't rate very highly, but it looked a bit like a little eye closing in sleep, and Herbert got used to saying good-night to it.

But even *he* thought he had reached desperate straits when he was reduced to bidding good-night to an electronic fade-out.

He watched the screen, quietly fanning his fins in the waterweeds. The next programme came on: "Teach Yourself Russian". Herbert swam close to the glass. The programme commenced. It was extremely interesting, and he became quite absorbed, especially so when he realised he had quite a gift for languages—Russian, anyway. By the end of that first morning's lesson, Herbert knew 'Da' and 'Nyet' and 'Tovarich'. He was really pleased.

He took a short nap afterwards and woke up in the afternoon. This time

there was a children's programme just starting.

Herbert swam closer and watched, as it looked very interesting. The programme was called "How To Semaphore", and a sailor demonstrated with flags how to signal all kinds of vital information under difficult circumstances. Herbert was enthralled. Obviously he had no flags, but this was a minor drawback to a Blotchy Great Snapper who was also Inventive. Herbert was quick to recognise the potential of being able to communicate, and waggled his pectoral and caudal fins reflectively. As flags they seemed to present no problems and, he mused, he was probably better equipped for the Royal Navy than most sailors.

After that, there was no holding him. The signalling was a tremendous success and he simply soaked up Russian. By the time the two series had ended, six weeks later, Herbert was proficient in English *and* Russian *and* in semaphoring in both languages. Then he took a short holiday and rested his brain.

Meantime, Mr. Hathaway had been busy too. There were all sorts of organisations which wanted him to appear with Herbert, and, as many of these were overseas, he made reservations for Herbert's tank and himself to travel in adjoining seats of the aircraft which was taking them firstly to America. There were lots of other things to arrange, but at last the day arrived when he went to the laboratory to collect Herbert.

He burst through the door full of vim and vigour. 'Come on, old boy!' he carolled. 'Today's the day! Adventure beckons and all that!'

'Does it indeed?' thought Herbert. 'And where have you been all this while I should like to know?'

'We must take your food and your extra waterweeds,' said Mr. Hathaway, and he took a large jar and scooped the weeds out of the bucket in which the lab. assistant kept them, and pushed handfuls into the jar, which he then topped up with water. He put the box of Herbert's ants' eggs into his pocket. He turned off the television. Then he picked up Herbert's tank and staggered with it out to the waiting taxi.

'Blimey!' said the taxi-driver. 'Is that the famous Herbert?'

'It is,' said Mr. Hathaway, depositing the tank on the back seat. 'Keep your fingers out if you know what's good for you!'

'Thank you very much,' thought Herbert, who liked juicy fingers. 'A great help you are. Always thinking of others.'

They made it to the airport in good time. Mr. Hathaway got help in carrying the tank into the aircraft, and, after a bit of heaving and shoving, Herbert was glad to find he was on the window side. It was really very good, as he could clearly see the wing from his vantage point and this, he thought, would add much interest to the journey which he suspected was going to be

a long one.

Mr. Hathaway and the other passengers prepared for the take-off. The air hostess came and smiled at Herbert.

'Isn't he *beautiful*?' she said admiringly.

'Yes,' thought Herbert.

'And isn't he *fat*?' she added, laughing.

'Watch it, Comrade,' thought Herbert, 'less of the personal stuff if you don't mind.'

Mr. Hathaway settled back in his seat. Herbert settled in his waterweeds. The plane lifted into the air and they were off. People relaxed, unfastened their seat belts, and began talking.

Herbert dozed for a bit as the motion of the plane was pleasant and he was comfortable, but eventually he woke and had a stretch and a look round. The passengers were all occupied with eating or crosswords and things like that, and Herbert was the only living thing to look idly out of the window.

He saw a wisp of smoke.

It came from under the wing near to where it joined the plane's body.

He watched carefully but the smoke continued in a thin trickle.

Herbert was nonplussed. Could this be right? If not, what should he do? Underneath them were the cold waters of the North Atlantic and, although

Herbert could regard the idea of a crash into the ocean with greater equanimity than the rest of the passengers, he was a river fish of parochial upbringing, and the thought of millions of tons of salty water occupied by millions of fish-eating fish did not appeal. So he jumped up and down and succeeded in thoroughly splashing Mr. Hathaway, which proved an effective way of attracting attention.

'Cut that out!' said Mr. Hathaway angrily. 'Look what you've done! My jacket is new, and I don't want you soaking it!'

'Look out of the window,' thought Herbert, 'and you will not worry about your jacket.'

'And stop jerking about!' added Mr. Hathaway. 'What's the matter with you? Have you gone crackers?'

'Look out of the window,' thought Herbert, 'and I will not be the only one going crackers. I can guarantee it.'

Just then Mr. Hathaway leaned across the tank to look at the sea, and he noticed the smoke which was increasing in volume quite rapidly.

'Ahh!' shrieked Mr. Hathaway. 'Ahhh! Look! Smoke!'

There was pandemonium. Everybody shouted and yelled and the air hostess came tearing in to calm them down, but things were getting very difficult when the Captain's voice came over the inter-com.

'Please keep calm, ladies and gentlemen,' he said, 'everything is under control. Will Mr. Hathaway please come to the flight-deck?'

Mr. Hathaway got up and rushed through to where the Captain was seated.

'What do you want me for?' he asked nervously.

'You're a scientist, aren't you?' said the Captain. 'Well, we've got a fire in the plane near the wing section, a leak in the pressurising and heating system, and we'll soon have a thumpin' great hole, so how about something scientific to help us out?'

'Is it too late to turn back?' asked Mr. Hathaway hopefully.

'We passed the point of no return over the North Pole.'

'It seems a naïve question,' said Mr. Hathaway, 'but have you tried the fire extinguishers?'

'We have,' answered the air hostess, 'and they're empty now. We've also used up all the water in the galley to feed the pressurising and heating sys-

tem, but it's still leaking.'

'Right,' said Mr. Hathaway decisively, 'half a mo.' Then he rushed to where Herbert was waiting and in no time he had organised a sort of bucket-chain, with the passengers passing water out of Herbert's tank in mugs and drinking glasses, where it was decanted into the heating system, with a small quantity used to wet rags and finally suppress the fire.

Everyone was beginning to celebrate, when Mr. Hathaway realised that they had sorted everything out except the leak—that they still stood a good chance of freezing to death.

'What do we do now?' he exclaimed, striking his forehead dramatically with his clenched fist.

'Cut out the histrionics for a start,' thought Herbert, 'and look at me'.

Carefully manoeuvering in the little water they had left him, Herbert signalled 'W', and, as he was causing quite a bit of commotion in the shallow water, the Captain noticed him. He watched with interest as Herbert, having gained attention, again signalled 'W' and then 'E' and 'E' again and then 'D' and 'S'.

'Weeds?' muttered the Captain dazedly, 'Weeds?'

'WEEDS!' yelled Mr. Hathaway, 'Of course! Good old Herbert!'

'Oh great,' thought Herbert, 'the penny's finally dropped.'

Mr. Hathaway gathered up all the water weeds he could and fed them, bit by bit, into the pressurising and heating system. The flow of water in the system conveyed them directly to the hole, where they lodged and effectively dammed the leak.

The aircraft steadied and then flew on with no more trouble. The passengers and crew were delighted with Mr. Hathaway and his incredible fish, and, when they realised that Herbert's water was a bit low for comfort, they opened a few bottles of champagne and topped him up.

Herbert spent the rest of the trip in a happy daze as he was definitely not accustomed to champagne, but, on reflection, he decided he could become used to it quite easily, and he kept thinking many joyful thoughts, until Mr. Hathaway's voice penetrated his mental fog.

'Yes,' Mr. Hathaway was saying smugly. 'First we go to New York, and then to Minnesota, and then we fly to Russia for the first showing of a Blotchy Great Snapper anywhere in the U.S.S.R.! The only drawback is my not speaking Russian!'

'Is it now?' thought Herbert. 'But I can understand Russki very well in-

deed, and unless I miss my guess (and I do not usually), it will not take yours truly very long to establish cordial relationships with our Soviet comrades. Then I will stir up the bortsch.'

When they landed at their destination, there was a Grand Ceremony in which Herbert was invested with the title of Captain, and a hat with the appropriate gold braid was hung on the corner of his tank. He made a fin semaphore which said 'Thanks—but pour in the champagne', and they all exclaimed how marvellous he was, and tipped in a whole magnum of Moët et Chandon. Herbert gulped and gulped, and finally sank down in a total stupor, but Mr. Hathaway said nothing. He had gone very quiet.

He had just noticed that in the gravel at the bottom of the tank someone had constructed, out of the coloured pebbles, a tiny little hammer-and-sickle sign, and he thought he knew who that someone was.

Mr. Hathaway suddenly had several nasty notions about Herbert; he expected a lot of trouble on their forthcoming travels.

Herbert opened one eye and grinned at Mr. Hathaway; Herbert expected trouble too. He was looking forward to making it!

CHAPTER 4

It was a beautiful spring day. The sun poured into the laboratory through the wide windows and warmed Herbert's tank up nicely.

He lay half-asleep in the waterweeds and day-dreamed quietly. All was peaceful. But not for long.

There came a pounding of feet, the door flew back and Mr. Hathaway, a picture of happiness, waltzed into the room.

'Russia!' he warbled. 'Little Mother Russia! Babushka, here we come!'

Herbert rose to the top of his tank and looked hard at Mr. Hathaway.

'Russia?' thought Herbert. 'Babushka yet? What *is* he on about now?'

'Hey, Herbert, old pal! We're off to Russia next week! How's about that? Our permits have come, and we can go on our visit! Ain't life grand?' And whistling 'The Volga Boatman' badly out of tune, Mr. Hathaway crashed out of the laboratory.

One week later they were on the plane to Moscow Airport. The journey was uneventful and Herbert slept most of the time.

They were met by a delegation of three large Russian Officials in extremely heavy overcoats and escorted to the hotel. Arrangements were made to take Mr. Hathaway and Herbert next day to an experimental Fish Farm, and there Mr. Hathaway would lecture to the students about Blotchy Great Snappers, using Herbert as his example. The three large Russians then left the two travellers to rest until morning.

Came the dawn. Also came a maid carrying a tray piled high with food. Now Mr. Hathaway was a bit of a pig and he was really looking forward to his first Russian breakfast, so he lost no time in getting out of bed to see what he had.

There was bortsch, which is beetroot soup, and bortsch at seven in the morning is *not* everybody's idea of a good thing. There were pancakes and a small pot of caviare, which looked like ball-bearings in sump-oil to the unhappy Mr. Hathaway. And there was tea. Only there wasn't any milk—just a dish of jam. And somebody had already poured out a glass—*not* a cup of tea and *then* they'd added plenty of jam and stirred it up well. It looked, thought Mr. Hathaway, like a glass of instant yuck. But as there was nothing else and he did not want to offend his hosts, poor Mr. Hathaway ate what he could and drank as little as possible.

He gave the caviare to Herbert, so fifty per cent of the party ate extremely well.

The large Russians arrived just as breakfast was finished. One of them was the interpreter and he smiled hugely at Mr. Hathaway.

'Did you like the food, Comrade? It was good, no?'

'N—oh, yes! Gosh, great! Really something!' Mr. Hathaway put on his coat and picked up Herbert's tank to hide his confusion. He did it very well.

Nobody noticed, except Herbert. And he wasn't saying anything.

They all went outside to where a small fleet of enormous black cars was waiting.

They headed for the Moskva River, and it was a big surprise to Mr. Hathaway to find that Moscow was not knee-deep in snow but, on the contrary, spring-time in Russia was much the same as spring-time anywhere else. The wind was chilly and made him shiver a bit, but Herbert in his tank on the back seat was quite comfortable.

They arrived at the Fish Farm. It was an imposing looking place with large buildings on the river and a whole lot of work in progress. They went to the reception area and met their hosts. Then the whole party went down to look at the river and Herbert went with them. He was taken by the most enormous Russian of them all—he carried Herbert's tank as if it were a jam jar.

When they reached the Moskva, the tank was put on the ground and Mr. Hathaway was treated to a long talk on how brilliant the work was that the Russian Scientists were doing. There wasn't a great deal about Blotchy Great Snappers, however, and both Herbert and Mr. Hathaway suspected that this was because Blotchy Great Snappers were even rarer in Russia than in England.

'No wonder they wanted me to come,' thought Herbert. 'I bet they've never even *seen* one like me before. What a backward lot they are.'

Just then, someone said something to the most enormous Russian of them all and he snapped smartly into a military salute as he replied. His foot caught Herbert's tank and, as quick as a flash, tank and contents shot down into the Moskva!

Nobody was more astonished than Herbert. One minute on the bank and the next in the cold, cold water. He wasn't used to it. Winter in the dear old river at home had been chilly, but this was even worse. He swam to the bottom to think about the situation.

Up on the bank, Mr. Hathaway was going mad. So were all the Officials. They were shouting and waving their arms in a very Russian manner. Mr. Hathaway hated them.

'Herbert has gone, and it's all thanks to you, you great Slavic idiot!' he yelled at the largest Russian. 'The most famous fish in the world is lost in your blasted river! Curse you all, you Russian blights!'

The interpreter did not interpret this to his friends. He didn't think it would be wise, so what he actually said was, 'Our English friend is much disturbed, Comrades. Let us drive down river and see if we can intercept this fish with a large net!'

They pushed Mr. Hathaway into a car and drove to an office, where they borrowed a huge net. Then they travelled down river and waited on the bank. The largest Russian had the net and he was crying his eyes out.

'It is so tragic!' he sobbed. 'So Russki in all the suffering! Poor little English fish! Doswidania, 'Erbert!'

They waited. They watched. A long time passed.

'Shut up, you Russian berk!' said Mr. Hathaway between his teeth.

They waited. They watched.

The interpreter said, 'Just up the river is the place where Ivan lost the jewels belonging to the Czarina. What a tragedy that was! The boat capsized with all the jewels on board and was never seen again! Ah, what grief!'

Mr. Hathaway scowled. 'What are you drivelling about? Ivan the Terrible

never lost any jewels that I ever heard of.'

'Not Ivan the Terrible,' answered the interpreter. 'It was his nephew, Ivan the Awful. He wasn't quite so bad as his uncle but he *did* steal the jewels of the Czarina. And they were never seen again—it was a terrible calamity!'

'Oh belt up!' retorted Mr. Hathaway. 'I don't care about your rotten jewels. Just you keep looking for Herbert!'

Herbert was in the mud, recovering from his shock. When he felt better he swam out. The river Moskva was not an inviting place. It was cold, dank and dreary.

Slowly Herbert swam off downstream. Where was Mr. Hathaway? Where was comfort and safety? He felt very homesick.

He swam round a huge boulder—suddenly there was a flicker of some-thing shiny in the weeds. Herbert paused to watch, and then the most incred-ible thing occurred. *Another* Blotchy Great Snapper slid out of its hiding place and looked at Herbert! It was the greatest moment of his life—he wasn't alone any more!

'Zdrastwuite, tovarich,' said the other fish softly.

'Same to you,' gulped Herbert, in fish, of course.

'Who are *you*, Comrade?' asked the silvery fish. 'I am Natasha Katerina and I have been very lonely for a long time. What is *your* name?'

'Herbert,' said Herbert. 'What are you doing here?'

'This is my home,' answered Natasha Katerina. 'But you are not Russian?'

'I should jolly well think not,' returned Herbert grimly. 'I'm used to something better than this crummy Russki river, I can tell you. Isn't it *dull*?'

'Oh, not *all* of it,' said Natasha Katerina, swishing her tail about. 'Follow me and I will show you something!'

And with that, she made off downstream. Herbert followed because it seemed like a good idea, but he was absolutely astounded when Natasha Katerina went through an opening in the river bank and inside, partly buried in mud, were the actual jewels of Ivan the Awful! Neither of the fishes knew to whom the jewels belonged, of course, but Herbert was bright enough to recognise good stuff when he saw it and it occurred to him that Mr. Hathaway would be absolutely delighted with all these sparkly things.

He nosed about until a tiara worked free of the mud then he turned to Natasha Katerina and said, 'Here, put this thing round your neck.'

'I haven't got a neck,' replied Natasha Katerina truthfully. 'What is that object, Comrade?'

'Oh, crikey. Just shove your head through until it's behind your gills. O.K.?' said Herbert.

She did and she looked really lovely.

Herbert's fishy heart went pit-a-pat, but he had no time for things like that. There was work to be done.

'Come on, now. Be careful and don't lose it,' Herbert said, as he led the way down the river.

Up on the bank, Mr. Hathaway kept looking. So did the Russian Officials. They didn't care for Mr. Hathaway's expression at all, so they were hoping

fervently that Herbert would show up. And he *did*!

Jumping in and out of the water like salmon came *two* Blotchy Great Snappers! Closer and closer they came and Mr. Hathaway held his breath. Could it possibly be Herbert?

Yes it *was*! Mr. Hathaway went even more mad. He grabbed the fish net and rushed to the water's edge. He leaned out as far as he could reach, and Herbert joyfully plopped into the net with Natasha Katerina close behind him. Oh, it was good to be safe again!

The Russians had organised a small tank complete with waterweeds, and Mr. Hathaway slid the two fishes into it. Then he noticed the tiara round Natasha Katerina. So did the Russians.

'What is *that*, Comrade?' asked the interpreter, pointing to the jewels. His

hand was shaking.

'I haven't the faintest idea,' returned Mr. Hathaway. 'Only look!' he added. 'We've got *another* Blotchy Great Snapper! I can't believe my luck! Good old Herbert, you really are the most amazing thing!'

'I certainly am,' thought Herbert, and he smiled with all his teeth at Natasha Katerina. She smiled back and she had just as many teeth as Herbert. He noticed this fact and made up his mind never to quarrel with his new friend. It would be too dangerous.

They were escorted back to the Fish Farm, where experts examined the tiara. 'The problem is—how do we find the rest of the treasure, Comrade?' asked the Director of the Fish Farm.

'We'll ask Herbert!' said Mr. Hathaway confidently.

All the Russians looked amazed. They knew the English were pretty potty, but asking a fish to direct them to buried treasure was surely over the top! Mr. Hathaway didn't care. He leaned over the smart new tank that Herbert and his friend had been given and he said, 'Now, old lad, tell us where the treasure is!' so Herbert did.

He signalled in perfect Russian exactly where the jewels were and the Officials—after they had got over the shock, which took a bit of time and a lot of vodka—acted on Herbert's instructions.

An expedition set out to search the river, and very soon the rest of Ivan the Awful's jewels had been recovered. Herbert was made a Hero of the Soviet Union and given a huge medal for which he signalled thanks.

Mr. Hathaway's tour was a triumphant one. Everywhere they went crowds of people gathered to see Herbert and his new comrade, and, as caviare was fed to them pretty constantly, both fishes were happy.

When the time came for Mr. Hathaway and Herbert to go home, a special visa was given to Natasha Katerina, and she was allowed to leave for England too. They were also presented with a whole crate of vodka to share between the three of them, so the flight home was an extremely cheerful one.

'Thish,' said Mr. Hathaway slowly and carefully, 'hash been a very shucksheshful trip, old Comrade-in-armsh!'

'That it has,' thought Herbert, well pleased that he was no longer alone in his tank.

'Indeed, Comrade, you are right,' thought Natasha Katerina, as she rocked gently in the waterweeds. 'England will be a lot warmer than that dreary old Moskva. And I have heard many interesting things happen there, too. I wonder if I can get to see Princess Diana?'

DRAGONSHEAD Patrick Winstone-Storer illustrated by Roz Wolseley-Charles

DRAGONSHEAD is a fantasy novel peopled with characters from the fourteenth century book, The Mabinogion; a Celtic version of the Arthurian legends. This is destined to become one of the funniest novels of 1984.

In Dragonshead, political intrigue and hypocrisy lead to a violent revolution, engineered by a devil-worshipping Bishop, whereby Princess Gorgina the Great, MA, (knight school karate expert and weighing-in at eighteen and one half stone) deposes her brother, King Bryn.

The deposed King and Queen, with their daughter, Gwen Alarch, enlist the aid of the cranky old magician, Merlin, and the alcoholic King of the North, King Dunarth. Add two medieval 'heavies' called The Devil-helping, Princess Gorgina's pet snake, Barry the Adder, and a river that runs backwards with the full moon and one has a very funny, highly original novel with the sort of literary depth rarely found in children's literature.